With thanks to my two guinea pigs . . .
Hannah and **Ellie**

First U.S. **e**dition 2005

Library of Congress Cataloging-in-Publication Data is a**V**ailable.

Library of Congress Catalog Card Number 2004062939

ISBN 0-7636-2886-7

10 9 8 7 6 5 4 3 2 1

Print**e**d in China

This book was typeset in Frutiger.
The illust**r**ations were created digitally.

Candlewick Press
2067 Massachusetts Avenue
Cambridge, Massachusetts 02140

visit us at www.candlewick.com

whatever

by william bee

CANDLEWICK PRESS
CAMBRIDGE, MASSACHUSETTS

This is Billy.

And this is Billy's dad.

Billy can be very difficult to please.

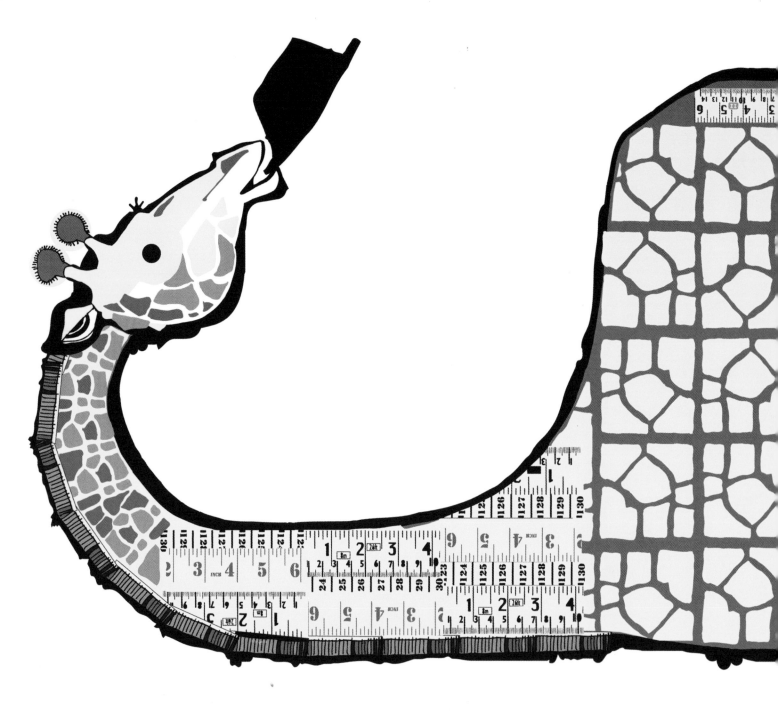

Show him something very tall . . . .

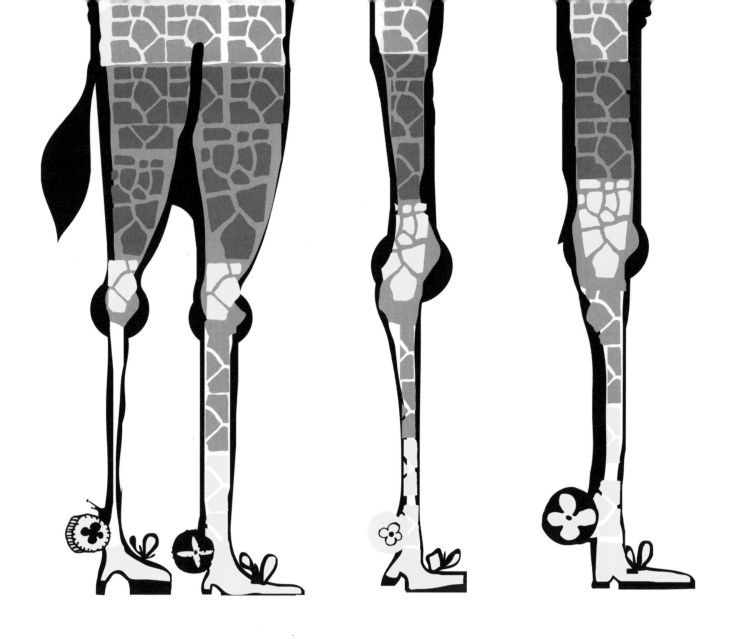

and he'll say **". . . whatever."**

Show him something very **small** . . .

and he'll say "... whatever."

Play him a tune on the world's **curliest** trumpet . . . and he'll say . . .

Fly him to the edge of outer space . . .
and he'll say . . .

". . . whatever."

And, when you try and scare him with the world's **hungriest** tiger . . . he'll say . . .

"Dad! I am still in here you know . . ."

"... whatever."